THE DOUBLE
OF MIRANDA TURNER

VOL. 1:
IF YOU HAVE GHOSTS

JAMIE S. RICH
Writer

GEORGE KAMBADAIS
Art & Colors

PAULINA GANUCHEAU
Colors (chapters 2 & 3)

CRANK!
Letterer/Book Design

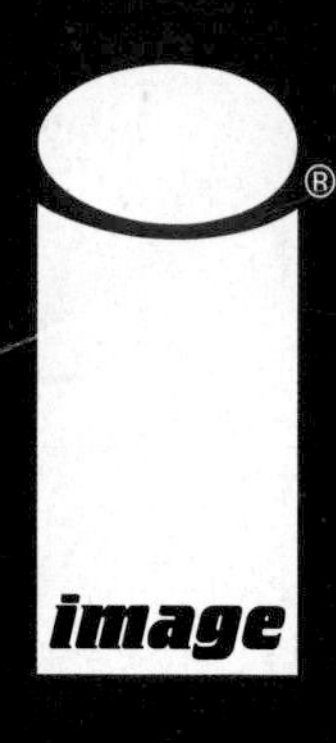

THE DOUBLE LIFE OF MIRANDA TURNER, VOL. 1: IF YOU HAVE GHOSTS. First printing. October 2016. Published by Image Comics, Inc. Office of publication: 2001 Center Street, Sixth Floor, Berkeley, CA 94704.

Originally published digitally by *Monkeybrain Comics*.
Special thanks to Chris Roberson and Allison Baker.

Color assist on chapter 1 by Mike Toris.

ISBN: 978-1-63215-924-3

CHAPTER 1:
SISTER WAS A ROLLING STONE

GEORGE KAMBADAIS - JAMIE S. RICH

THE DOUBLE LIFE OF MIRANDA TURNER

THE DOUBLE LIFE OF MIRANDA TURNER
"Sister Was a Rolling Stone"
written by Jamie S. Rich
Illustrated by George Kambadais
colors by Mike Toris and George Kambadais
letters by Crank!
MY SISTER ALWAYS WANTED TO BE AN ACTRESS WHEN SHE GREW UP.
I SUPPOSE IF YOU LOOK AT IT A CERTAIN WAY, THAT'S EXACTLY WHAT SHE HAS BECOME.
IT'S JUST THE ROLE THAT WOULD MAKE A NAME FOR HER TURNED OUT TO BE DIFFERENT FROM WHAT SHE EXPECTED.
SMASH
DANG IT!
THE MORE I SMASH...
...THE MORE THERE ARE!
KRSH
THAT'S MIRANDA THERE. ACTING LIKE A PROFESSIONAL CRIMEFIGHTER.

HER FOES TODAY AREN'T PLAYING.
HEH HEH HEH!
THEIR NOM-DE-CRIME IS "THE BLOCKHEADS."
THAT'S IT!
I'M GOING TO THE SOURCE!
MIRANDA CALLS HERSELF "THE CAT."
YIPE!
ZOOP
SHE HASN'T BEEN DOING IT AS LONG AS THEY HAVE.
TOO SLOW, KITTY-CAT!
GRRRR...
AND I WAS DOING IT LONGER THAN ALL THREE OF THEM COMBINED.

BACK WHEN I WAS THE CAT.
MIRANDA!
BACK BEFORE I WAS MURDERED.
GOOD THING NO ONE ELSE CAN HEAR YOU, LINDY.
YOU'RE TERRIBLE AT THE WHOLE SECRET IDENTITY THING.
GOTCHA!
"WHO SAYS? YOU NEVER KNEW I WAS THE CAT.
"BESIDES, IF YOU WERE WORRIED ABOUT BEING FOUND OUT, YOU WOULDN'T BE HERE.
"IT'S ONLY A MATTER OF TIME BEFORE SOMEONE FROM THE ALPHABET SHOWS UP TO FIGHT THESE JERKS."

WHICH ONLY MEANS I HAVE TO STOP THE BLOCKHEADS *BEFORE* THAT HAPPENS.

YOU TAKING CARE OF HER?
SHE'S TAKEN CARE OF.
OOF
BONK
OW!

HEE HEE HEE!
WHOOSH

YOU OKAY?
YEAH. I JUST HATE THOSE GUYS.
I HATE THEM SO MUCH!
WHAM
GREAT. MAKE A BIGGER MESS.
YOU REALIZE THEY CAN GENERATE THE BLOCKS FASTER THAN YOU CAN DESTROY THEM?
SO WHAT?
SO MAYBE YOU SHOULD LISTEN TO ME FOR A CHANGE.
LET A REAL SUPERHERO TAKE CARE OF THE BLOCKHEADS.

NO WAY. I CAN DO THIS.
I JUST HAVE TO FIGURE OUT HOW.
LOOKS LIKE THAT GIRL IN THE COSTUME FINALLY GAVE UP.
SHE LOOKED DIFFERENT TO YOU, TOO?

YEAH, SHE CALLS HERSELF "THE CAT"...
...BUT SHE'S NOT LIKE THE ONE IN THE PAPERS.
RIGHT.

NO MATTER. SOON EVERYTHING IN THIS CITY WILL LOOK DIFFERENT...
...SOMETHING MORE SUITED TO OUR PARTICULAR *ANGLE*.
VRRRTT
KRK

ARE YOU ALL RIGHT?
DON'T MOVE HIM!
HE MIGHT HAVE HURT HIS NECK!

HE'S MOVING FINE ON HIS OWN.
JUST NEEDS A LITTLE HELP.
YES, HE IS. YES, HE DOES.
GET YOURSELF SOME COVER, MAN.

WHAT ARE YOU DOING?
I HAVE AN IDEA.

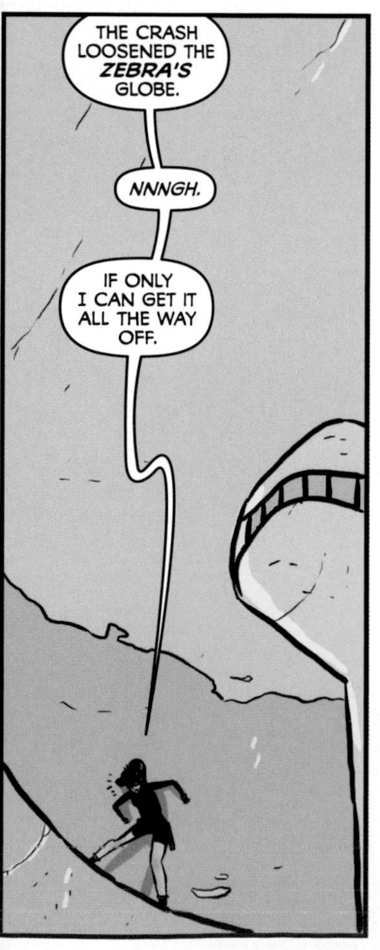
THE CRASH LOOSENED THE *ZEBRA'S* GLOBE.
NNNGH.
IF ONLY I CAN GET IT ALL THE WAY OFF.

THAT THING MUST WEIGH A TON.
YOU CAN PUT ON MY COSTUME, BUT THAT DOESN'T GIVE YOU SUPER POWERS.

YOU CAN'T BE THE CAT WITHOUT THE MYSTIC RUNE.
WELL, *MAYYYYYBE*
HUFF
IF YOU HADN'T LET YOURSELF BE MURDERED SO THE RUNE COULD BE
GNNN
STOLEN...

POP!
AH-HA!
RRRRUMMMBBBBLE
I TOLD YOU, DUDE. WE LAY ENOUGH BLOCKS, AND THIS CITY IS OURS.
KRK
SMSH
SURE, SURE. BUT NOW THAT WE HAVE IT...

...WHAT DO WE DO WITH IT?
DO YOU HEAR SOMETHING?
BOOSH
BOOM
AIEEE!
RIGHT DOWN THE CENTER!
WHAT THE HECK--?!
KABLOOEY

WOO-HOO!
THAT WAS AMAZING!
OKAY, I ADMIT, THAT WAS PRETTY GREAT.
BUT YOU'D BETTER JUMP OFF!
RRRRUMMM

JUMP OFF WHERE?
NOW THAT WE CLEARED THROUGH THOSE BLOCKS, THIS THING IS PICKING UP SPEED!
MMMBBBLLL

LLLRRRR
GYAHHHH!

I CAN'T LOOK.

WHOOPS.
SLAM

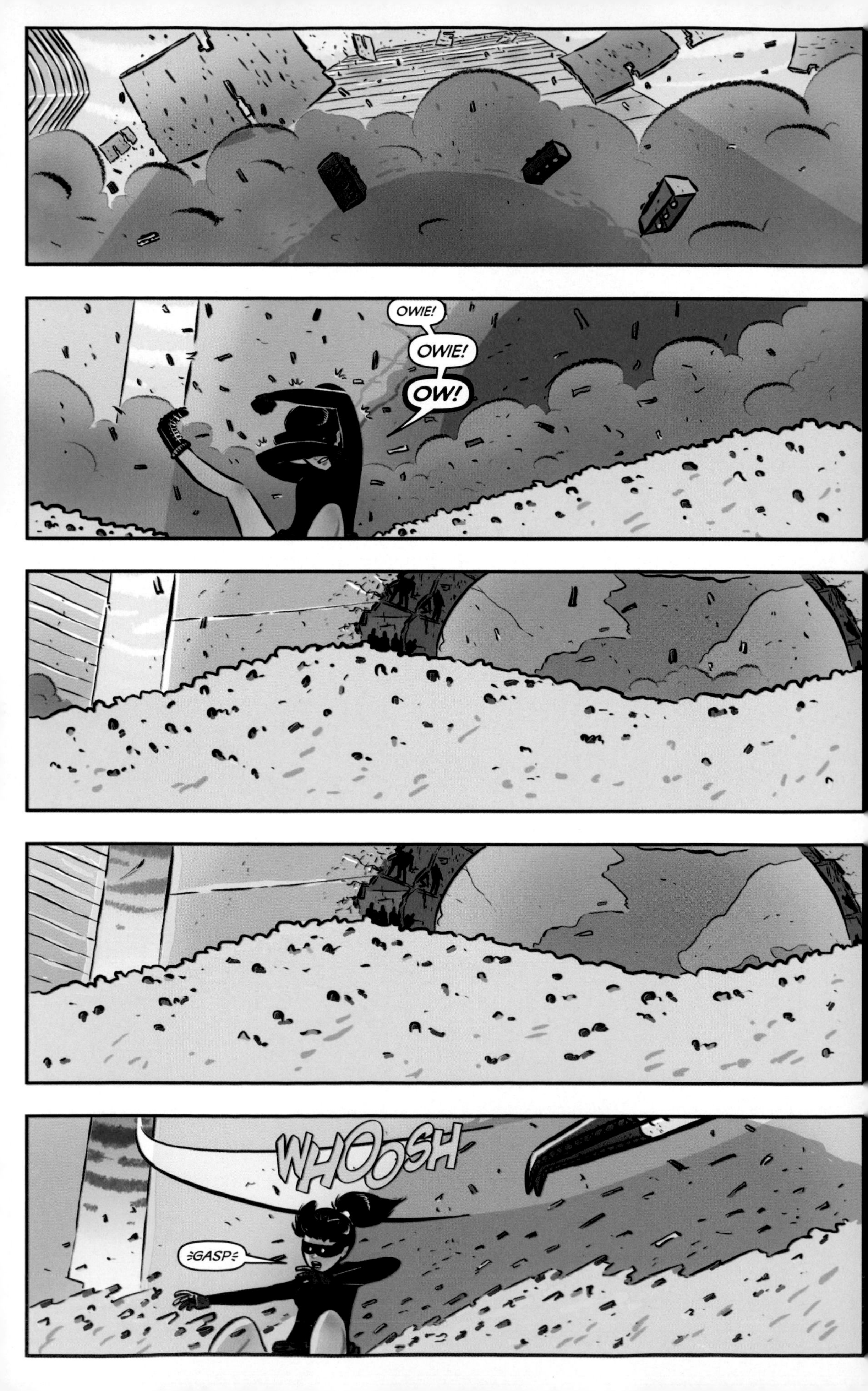
OWIE!
OWIE!
OW!
WHOOSH
GASP

I'LL SHOW THAT LITTLE BRAT WHAT'S WHAT.
WHILE YOU DO THAT, I'LL GIVE HER THE WHAT FOR.
GENTLEMEN...
SEEING AS HOW YOU LIKE SQUARES SO MUCH...
...HOW ABOUT I SHOW YOU A SIX-BY-SIX FOOT CELL BLOCK?

ARE YOU KIDDING ME?
THE ZEBRA FLIES IN AT THE LAST MINUTE AND TAKES ALL THE CREDIT?
CONSIDER YOURSELF LUCKY...
...THIS WAY HE NEVER REALIZES IT WASN'T ME IN THE COSTUME, AND THE GUILD LEAVES YOU ALONE FOR ANOTHER DAY.
I GUESS.
AND YOU KNOW, IT WAS HIS STATUE THAT SAVED THE DAY.
I JUST GAVE IT A PUSH.
HOW IS IT, AGAIN, THAT I'M THE ONE WHO'S DEAD?
I'D NEVER TELL HER THIS, BUT MY SISTER ISN'T SO BAD AT BEING A CRIMEFIGHTER.
LET'S JUST HOPE SHE DOESN'T FORGET WHAT WE'RE DOING THIS FOR.
BECAUSE WHOEVER WANTED TO KILL THE PREVIOUS CAT MIGHT WANT THE NEW CAT DEAD, AS WELL.

Chapter 2:
If You Have Ghosts, Part 1

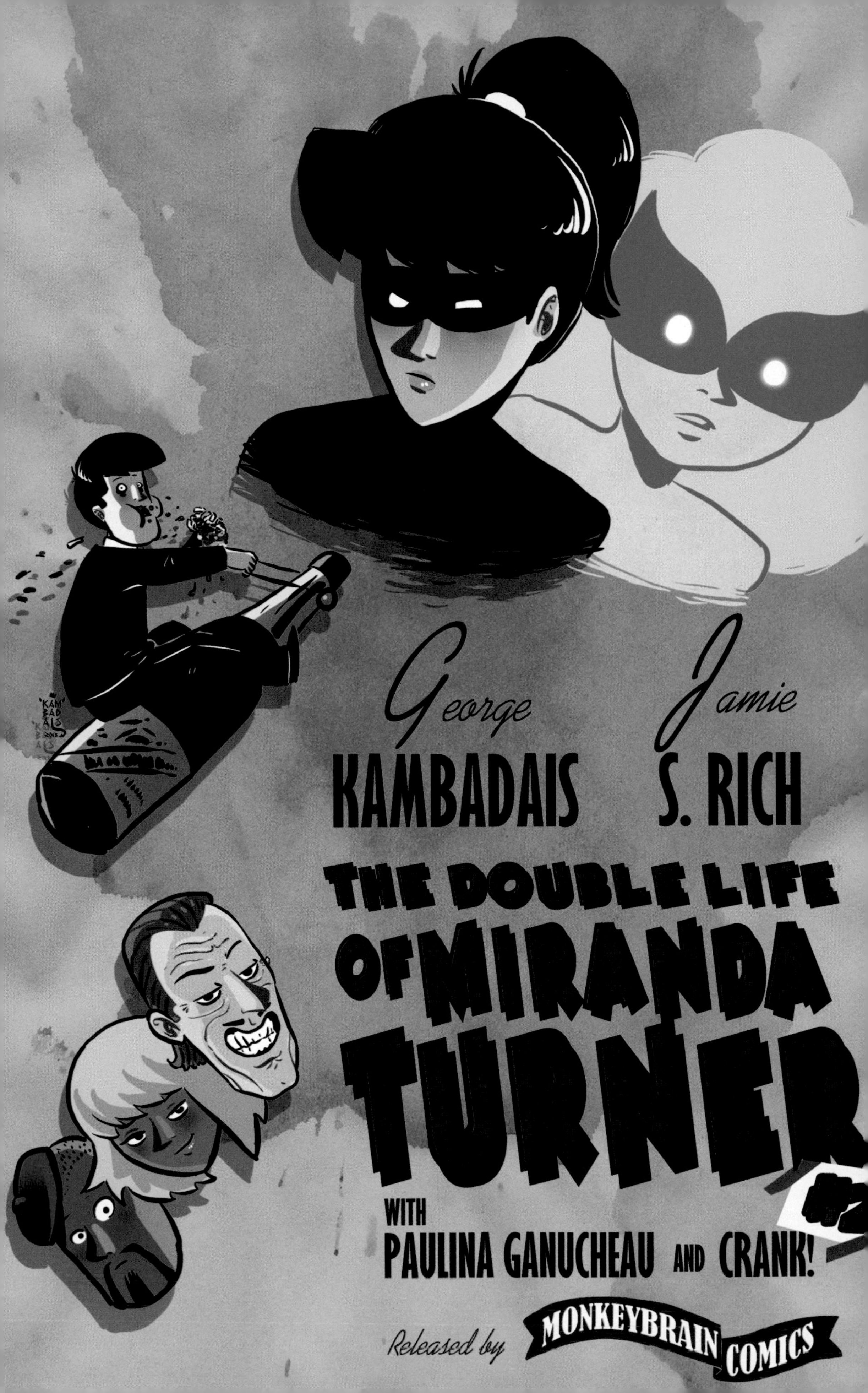
George KAMBADAIS
Jamie S. RICH
THE DOUBLE LIFE OF MIRANDA TURNER
WITH PAULINA GANUCHEAU AND CRANK!
Released by MONKEYBRAIN COMICS

OH, GEORGE, YOU'RE GETTING TRANSPARENT.
YOU'RE...YOU'RE FADING.
SAY, THAT'S FUNNY...
...I CAN SEE THROUGH YOU, TOO.

YOU KNOW SOMETHING, GEORGE?
I-I THINK WE'RE DEAD.

IT'S FUNNY, I DON'T FEEL ANY DIFFERENT.

CUT!

WHAT'S THE MATTER, HAL?
I THOUGHT WE DID PRETTY GOOD THAT TIME.
IT'S NOT YOU, ARCHIE.
IT'S YOUR MAKEUP.

THE DOUBLE LIFE OF MIRANDA TURNER
"IF YOU HAVE GHOSTS, PART 1"
WRITTEN BY JAMIE S. RICH
ART BY GEORGE KAMBADAIS
COLORS BY PAULINA GANUCHEAU
LETTERS BY CRANK!
MOON, WHERE'S YOUR HEAD AT?!
WHY, WHATEVER DO YOU MEAN, MAESTRO?
THE GHOSTLY EFFECT LOOKS MAGNIFICENT WHEN THE HOUSE LIGHTS GO DOWN.

SURE, IT LOOKS GREAT. UNTIL HE HOLDS UP HIS HANDS!
THEN IT'S GOOD-BYE ***ECTOPLASM***, HELLO ***PIGMENT!***

I DON'T UNDERSTAND. I KNOW I DIDN'T FORGET.
I APPLIED HIS HAND MAKEUP LAST.
IT'S TRUE, I SAW IT.

I GIVE UP!
EVERYBODY TAKE TEN AND GET IT TOGETHER WHILE YOU DO.

SORRY ABOUT THAT, MOON.
I HAD TO TAKE A LEAK AND, YOU KNOW, CLEANLINESS BEING NEXT TO GOD AND ALL.
WELL, AT LEAST NOW I KNOW I'M NOT GOING SENILE.

ARCHIE, YOU JERK!
WHY DID YOU LET HIM TAKE THE BLAME FOR YOU?
COME ON, I'M SECOND BILLED IN THIS THING.
I'M JUST LOOKIN' OUT FOR ME.

IT'S ALL RIGHT, MS. TURNER.
THE TALENT COMES FIRST.

YOU'RE CALLING *HIM* "TALENT"?
HEY!
HEE-HEE-HEE.

YOU KNOW, MS. TURNER, I WORKED WITH YOUR SISTER ONCE.
I STYLED HER FOR A MAGAZINE SHOOT.

IS IT TRUE SHE RETIRED?
UM, IN A MANNER OF SPEAKING...

WELL, I'LL RESPECT LINDY'S PRIVACY AND NOT ASK WHERE SHE'S GONE.
I'D HATE TO DISTURB WHATEVER PEACE SHE'S FOUND.

WELL, MY GHOST GETUP IS ALL GOOD, SO I'M GOING TO MAKE THE MOST OF THIS BREAK.
SEE YOU IN A FEW.

YES, SEE YOU SOON.
YEAH, DON'T BE LATE.

SOMEONE MIGHT HAVE OUR HEAD IF WE BLOW IT AGAIN.
YES.
AGAIN.

YOU KNOW, *LINDY*...
...I BET I'M THE ONLY PERSON WHO'S EVER BEEN IN THIS PLAY THAT HAD AN ACTUAL GHOST FOLLOWING HER AROUND.
I SUPPOSE IT'S KIND OF IRONIC.

I *WISH*, HOWEVER, THAT YOU WERE OUT LOOKING FOR MY KILLER.
NOT SPENDING YOUR TIME RUNNING LINES.

I'M AN ACTRESS. I NEED TO ACT.
BESIDES, YOU'RE THE ONE WHO KEEPS PUSHING ME TO DIAL BACK THE CRIMEFIGHTING.

THIS ISN'T WHAT I MEANT.

WELL, EITHER WAY, IT'S NOT LIKE I SHOULD HAVE TO GIVE UP MY LIFE TO BE A MASKED HERO.
YOU WERE STILL A MODEL WHEN YOU WERE *THE CAT.*

TRUE. IT PROVIDED ME GOOD COVER.
I COULD TAKE GIGS ALL OVER THE WORLD AND USE MY CELEBRITY TO GET OUT OF EXPLAINING WHY I WAS OFTEN PLACES I DIDN'T BELONG.

THE FUNNY THING ABOUT BEING AN INTERNATIONAL ADVENTURER...
MINE!

...IS TROUBLE FINDS YOU.
ALL =GLRFFLE= MINE!

YO, ARCHIE, EASE UP ON THE SNACK TRAY, MAN.
NO! GET AWAY!
NOT YOURS, MINE!
EVERYTHING MINE.
WHAT'S GOTTEN INTO HIM?

BEATS ME.
BUT SOMETHING'S NOT RIGHT HERE.
"DUE TO UNFORESEEN EVENTS..."

...ARCHIE WILL NOT BE RETURNING TO THE PRODUCTION.
EVEN IF THEY REMOVED THE PSYCH HOLD, HE'D STILL HAVE TO FACE THEFT CHARGES.

LIEV HAS BEEN SERVING AS ARCHIE'S STAND-IN, AND HE'LL TAKE OVER THE ROLE OF GEORGE.
HELLO, ALL.

DID THEY EVER FIND THE JEWELS ARCHIE STOLE?
NOPE.

THEY THINK HE MAY HAVE HAD AN ACCOMPLICE THAT HE DUMPED THEM WITH.
HE JUST CHARGED INTO THE STORE AND STARTED TAKING STUFF.

THIS REMINDS ME OF A PRODUCTION OF *CUCKOO'S NEST* WE DID BACK IN '72--
GIVE US A BREAK, OLD MAN.
NO ONE CARES ABOUT YOUR STORIES FROM THE LAST CENTURY.

ALL RIGHT, *GINA*. THAT'S ENOUGH OF THAT.
JUST BE ON ALERT...

"...AND LOOK OUT FOR ONE ANOTHER."
THE STORE ARCHIE ROBBED WAS JUST ACROSS THE STREET.
AND THE POLICE NABBED HIM A BLOCK AWAY.

THAT DOESN'T LEAVE A LOT OF PLACES FOR HIM TO STASH THE LOOT.
AAIEEEEEEE!
WHAT WAS THAT?
I DON'T KNOW...
...BUT *THE CAT* IS GOING TO FIND OUT.
G-GINA?!
SHUSH, ROOKIE.
THE CAT DOESN'T KNOW GINA.

WH-WHAT HAPPENED TO ME?!
I'M OLD!

MA'AM, I DON'T...I DON'T KNOW WHO YOU ARE.
BUT YOU'RE GOING TO HAVE TO STAY CALM.
NICE COVER.

HOW DID THIS HAPPEN?
I'M TWENTY-TWO YEARS OLD. I HAVE A STRICT SKIN-CARE REGIMEN.
MAYBE IT'S AN ALLERGIC REACTION...?

OH, MY GOD.
MY ENDORSEMENT DEALS!
HOW CAN I DO COMMERCIALS FOR ACNE CREAM LOOKING LIKE THIS?

TAKE CONTROL OF THE SITUATION, MIRANDA.
ASK HER WHAT SHE WAS DOING BEFORE SHE DISCOVERED THIS CHANGE.
WHAT WERE YOU DOING BEFORE YOU WENT ALL SENIOR CITIZEN?

SMOOTH. YOU'VE GOT A REAL WAY WITH WORDS, SIS.
I DON'T KNOW. I...I HAD COME IN HERE TO TAKE A NAP.
THEN THERE WAS A KNOCK AT THE DOOR--

WHAM
YOU MEAN LIKE THAT?
NOT EXACTLY.
BAWHAM
IT WASN'T QUITE SO LOU*UAAHHHHH!*
KRCK

GARRRRHHHH!
BREAK TIME IS OVER!
BNK
I'M SICK OF ALL YOUR YELLING.
TRY USING YOUR INSIDE VOICE.

THIS IS A CLOSED REHEARSAL.
SWACK
AND YOU'RE WANTED IN WARDROBE!
NO!

YOU'VE GOT A LEGIT ANGER MANAGEMENT PROBLEM, FELLA.
SWP
GRRRRRRRR.
UH-OH.

RARRRHHH!
SEE?
THIS IS EXACTLY WHAT I WAS TALKING ABOUT!
KRASH

CHAPTER 3:
IF YOU HAVE GHOSTS, PART 2

GEORGE KAMBADAIS - JAMIE S. RICH
THE DOUBLE LIFE
OF MIRANDA
TURNER
#3

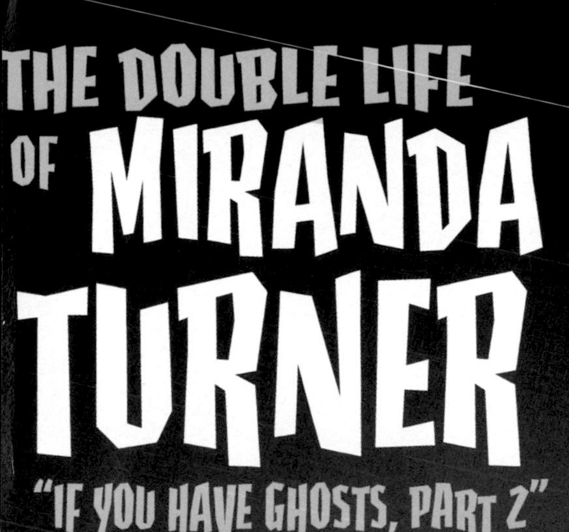

"IF YOU HAVE GHOSTS, PART 2"

WRITTEN BY JAMIE S. RICH

ART BY GEORGE KAMBADAIS

COLORS BY PAULINA GANUCHEAU

LETTERS BY CRANK!

THIS IS MY WORLD, MY STAGE.

IT'S BEST FOR ALL OF US WHEN YOU DO WHAT I SAY.

WAKE UP, *MIRANDA*.
YOU NEED TO MOVE BEFORE HE HITS YOU AGAIN!

EVERYONE TAKE FIVE.

OOF.
CRIMEFIGHTING IS MURDER ON THE SPINE.

HM?

ON SECOND THOUGHT, STAY DOWN.
PLAY DEAD.

LET THE ANGRY BEAR MOVE ALONG.

BUT, *LINDY*, WE NEED TO STOP HIM.
WHAT IF HE STARTS BEATING ON OTHER PEOPLE?
I THINK HIS VINEGAR IS RUNNING DRY.

BUT YOU'RE RIGHT.
I'LL STAY ON HIS TRAIL TO MAKE SURE.
MEANWHILE...

"...YOU NEED TO STOP BEING *THE CAT* AND GO BACK TO BEING YOURSELF. SEE WHAT YOU CAN FIND OUT FROM THE REST OF THE CAST."
THERE'S NO WAY AROUND IT.
THIS PRODUCTION IS CURSED!

I KNOW WE'RE *ACTORS*, BUT LET'S NOT BE *DRAMATIC*, GINA.
SCREW YOU, *LIEV*, YOU DON'T LOOK LIKE SOMEBODY'S GRANDMOTHER.

THE ONLY REASON *YOU'RE* NOT UPSET IS BECAUSE ARCHIE GOING ALL LOONEY MEANS YOU GOT HIS PART.
HEY, THAT'S TRUE!

YOU'RE THE ONLY ONE HERE TO BENEFIT FROM ALL THESE CRAZY GOINGS-ON.
IF YOU'RE IMPLYING I HAVE SOMETHING TO DO WITH THEM...

...THEN WHY WOULD I KEEP GOING AND RISK US GETTING SHUT DOWN?
IT DOESN'T MAKE SENSE.
DANG IT.
THAT'S TRUE, TOO.

STILL, IT STANDS TO REASON THAT SOMEONE IS BEHIND THIS.
SOMEONE HAS SOMETHING TO GAIN FROM SABOTAGE.

"THE QUESTION IS...WHO?"
EASY THERE, BIG FELLA.

SOMEONE'S RUNNING OUT OF STEAM.

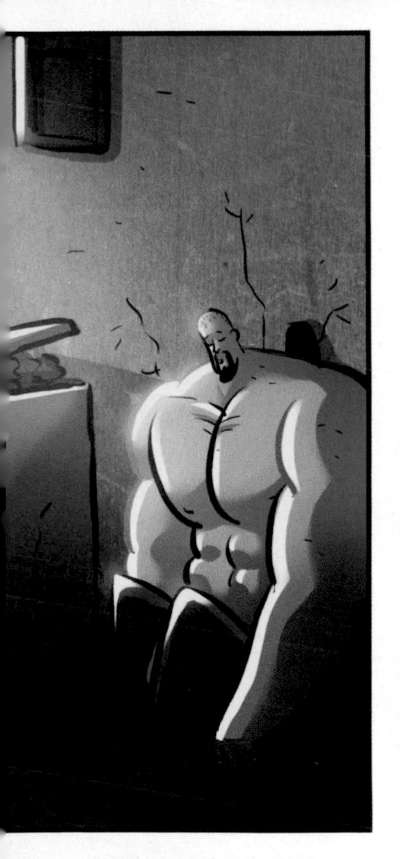

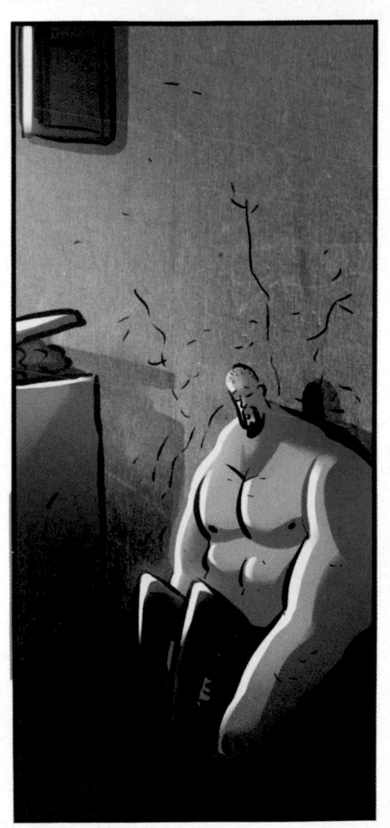

I WISH I COULD TOUCH YOU.
IT LOOKS LIKE THERE'S SOMETHING ON YOUR SKIN. IT MAY JUST BE SWEAT...

...BUT IT WAS THICKER.
LIKE IT WAS CAKED ON.
DO YOU THINK HE KNEW WHAT HE WAS DOING? BECAUSE I DON'T THINK ARCHIE DID.

EVEN IF THEY DID, SOMETHING TRIGGERED THEM BOTH.
THE WAY THE DIRECTOR CRASHED OUT LIKE THAT, IT WAS LIKE SOMETHING HAD PASSED FROM HIM.

WHICH TELLS US IT'S NOT PERMANENT.

AT LEAST NOT FOR EVERYBODY.
HANG ON A SECOND, I WANT TO CHECK SOMETHING.

FINE. IT'S NOT LIKE I HAVE ANYTHING ELSE TO DO BUT SIT HERE.

NOT TRUE!

I WANT TO DO SOME TESTS FOR YOUR GHOST MAKEUP.

OKAY.
BUT I THOUGHT WE HAD THAT ALL SET?
WE DID, BUT I HAVE SOME NEW PRODUCT.

IT'S A SPECIAL BLEND.

SOMEONE REALLY HIT YOU WHERE YOU LIVE, DIDN'T THEY, HONEY?

YOU DON'T KNOW HOW NOT TO BE BEAUTIFUL, SURROUNDED BY BEAUTIFUL THINGS.
SPEAKING OF WHICH...
...WHERE DID THAT SHINY BAUBLE COME FROM?
I'VE NEVER TRIED THIS BEFORE, BUT...
...I WONDER IF THERE'S ROOM FOR ME IN THAT EMPTY LITTLE HEAD OF YOURS?
WELL...
...HERE GOES NOTHING.

KNOK KNOK
OH, WHAT NOW?

WHAT DO YOU WANT, OLD MAN MOON?
COME NOW, IS THAT ANY TONE TO ADOPT...

...WITH A GENTLEMAN BEARING GIFTS?

I HOPE NOW WE CAN MAYBE... GET ALONG A LITTLE BETTER?

FAT CHANCE, MOON.
IT'S A GIFT, AND GIFTS SHOULDN'T HAVE STRINGS ATTACHED.

THAT'S AN UNFORTUNATE WAY OF LOOKING AT THINGS...
...*LITTLE GIRL*.

OH MY GOSH, *MIRANDA!*
I KNOW WHO THE CULPRIT IS.

IT'S MOON! ARCHIE GAVE HIM THE STOLEN JEWELS--
UH-OH.
JUST SIT STILL, MY DEAR.

NOT THAT YOU HAVE MUCH CHOICE.
YOU'LL FIND MY NEW FORMULA HAS LEFT YOU QUITE PARALYZED.

AFTER ALL, WE CAN'T HAVE *THE CAT* GETTING WISE TO MY SCHEMES.

OH, YES, I KNOW YOU'RE THE CAT.
I KNEW THE MOMENT I SAW YOU ON THE STREET FIGHTING WITH THE DIRECTOR.

I CAN'T WORK ON A FACE AS CLOSELY AS I HAVE YOURS AND NOT RECOGNIZE THOSE CHEEKBONES.
MASK OR NO MASK.

I DON'T THINK SO.
SWAT
WHAT? HOW--?!
NEVER MIND THAT.
IT'S YOU WHO GOT ARCHIE TO STEAL THOSE JEWELS, WHICH MEANS YOU PUSHED HIM OVER THE DEEP END, TOO.
THEN GINA REJECTED YOU WHEN YOU GAVE HER THE NECKLACE, SO YOU MADE HER OLD.
THERE'S NO WAY YOU COULD KNOW.
EVEN *SHE* DOESN'T KNOW.
IT'S YOUR MAKEUP, ISN'T IT?
YOU HAVE SOME SPECIAL RECIPE, IT CHANGES PEOPLE, MAKES THEM DO THINGS.
DID IT MAKE GINA FORGET?

YOU USED IT FOR PETTY REVENGE ON PEOPLE WHO ANNOYED YOU.
LET'S SAY I START EXPERIMENTING AND SEE WHAT KIND OF REVENGE I CAN GET.
NO! PLEASE!
I CAN GIVE YOU SOMETHING. INFORMATION.
INFORMATION ABOUT HOW LINDY WAS KILLED.
WHAT? WHAT DO YOU KNOW ABOUT MY--
--ABOUT *HER* MURDER?
I'M AN ACCOMPLICE.

YOU'RE RIGHT. MY MAKEUP ALTERS PEOPLE. IT EXAGGERATES THEIR WORST TRAITS.
OR IT WORKS LIKE MIND CONTROL.

BUT IT CAN ALSO ALTER YOUR APPEARANCE.
THE PERSON WHO KILLED YOU DIDN'T WANT YOU TO SEE THEIR REAL FACE.

WHO WAS IT? WAS IT A MAN? A WOMAN?
I COULDN'T SEE.
BZZT BZZZT

TAKE IT EASY. HE CAN'T HEAR YOU.
I WOULDN'T BE SO SURE.
BZZT BZZZT

HELLO? HOW DID...?
I SWEAR I DIDN'T TELL THEM ANYTHING. I DON'T KNOW ANYTHING.

WAIT. IS THAT THE KILLER?
GIVE ME THAT PHONE!
NO, I ASSURE YOU, THAT'S NOT NECESS--

GRK!

"CALL DISCONNECTED."
DID THE BAD GUY JUST KILL OLD MAN MOON OVER THE PHONE?
IT APPEARS SO...

WHOEVER IT IS HAS A GREATER REACH THAN WE REALIZED.
THEY AREN'T THE ONLY ONE.
WERE YOU INSIDE MY BODY MOVING ME AROUND?
YES.
I DIDN'T KNOW YOU COULD *DO* THAT!
NEITHER DID I.

I TRIED IT ON A HUNCH.
IT WAS KIND OF COOL, BUT KIND OF CREEPY AT THE SAME TIME.

YOU SHOULD SEE IT FROM MY SIDE.
I WAS IN GINA EARLIER.
NOW I ***REALLY*** DON'T LIKE THE WAY ***THAT*** SOUNDS.

Chapter 4:
That's How You Got Killed Before

GEORGE KAMBADAIS - JAMIE S. RICH

THE DOUBLE LIFE OF ~~MIRANDA~~ LINDY TURNER

#4

KAMBADAIS 2014

HIT THE LIGHTS.

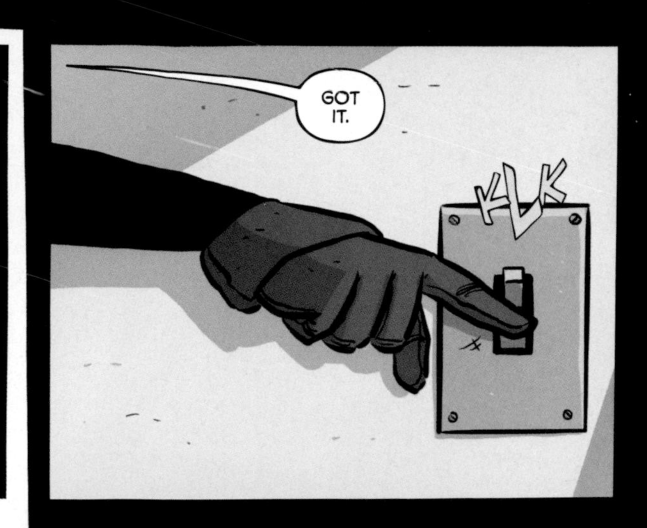

I'VE HEARD OF MURDERERS RETURNING TO THE SCENE OF THE CRIME...

HE DOUBLE LIFE
OF MIRANDA
URNER

"That's How You Got Killed Before"

Written by Jamie S. Rich

Art by George Kambadais

etters by Crank!

GIVEN THE NEW INFORMATION WE GOT FROM OLD MAN MOON...
...IT SEEMED LIKE A GOOD TIME TO GO OVER EVERYTHING ABOUT MY DEATH AGAIN.
HE DIDN'T TELL US MUCH.
ON THE CONTRARY, HE TOLD US A LOT.
BECAUSE NOW WE KNOW...
"...THE KILLER ALTERED HIS OR HER FACE, I HADN'T MENTALLY BLOCKED IT OUT.
"THE BLANK FEATURES WERE A RESULT OF MOON'S MAKEUP."

WE'LL ADD THAT TO HIS IMPRESSIVE LIST OF RESOURCES.
ALONGSIDE WHATEVER HE HAD THAT ALLOWED HIM TO FIND OUT WHO YOU WERE AND GET INTO YOUR LAIR.
BARELY ANY MEMBERS OF THE ALPHABET GUILD EVEN KNEW MY SECRET IDENTITY.
YET, THE KILLER CLEARLY KNEW ABOUT THE GUILD.
GIVEN THAT HE KNEW TO STEAL YOUR MYSTIC RUNE AND TAKE YOUR CAT POWERS.
EXACTLY.

"LET'S TRACE BACK OVER YOUR TIMELINE FOR THAT NIGHT AGAIN."
"OKAY, IT HAD BEEN A RATHER LONG DAY, STARTING WITH A PHOTOSHOOT..."
GOOD, GOOD!
THAT'S IT!
"IRONICALLY, IT WAS A JOB PLAYING COPS AND ROBBERS."
OKAY WE GOT WHAT WE NEEDED, SO DO SOMETHING DIFFERENT.
WHATEVER COMES TO MIND.
SURPRISE ME!
BANG.
BA--?!
CHOP
HYAH!
OWWWWW.
WHAT THE HELL, LINDY?
SORRY.
IT WAS JUST A REFLEX.

I DON'T LIKE GUNS.
"SO, THAT ENDED AWKWARDLY."

"YOU WENT HOME AFTER THAT, RIGHT?"
"BRIEFLY. I HAD TO CHANGE FOR AN EDUCATION FUNDRAISER I WAS DUE AT THAT EVENING."

"DID YOU COME INTO THE CAT'S LAIR?"
"YES. TO LOG ON AND SEE IF THERE WERE ANY GUILD BULLETINS.
"THE ROOM WAS EMPTY THEN. HAD ANYONE BEEN HERE, I'D HAVE NOTICED."

"WERE THERE ANY BULLETINS?"
"UH-HUH. MY ARCH FOE TENGU HAD ESCAPED FROM PRISON.
"I WAS TO BE ON THE LOOKOUT."

"COULD HE BE YOUR KILLER? HE SEEMS THE OBVIOUS CHOICE."
"IT'S POSSIBLE, BUT I CAN'T IMAGINE HIM NOT TAKING CREDIT FOR IT.
"THAT'S NOT HIS STYLE.

"BESIDES, LATER THAT NIGHT, HE GOT IN A TUSSLE WITH *PORTAL* OVER THE CONTENTS OF A BANK VAULT."
"EXCEPT SHE DIDN'T APPREHEND HIM, DID SHE?"
"NO. HE'S STILL AT LARGE."
SAY, ARE OTHER HEROES SUPPOSED TO GET INVOLVED WITH SOMEONE ELSE'S NEMESIS LIKE THAT?
SURE, IT'S NOT AN EXCLUSIVE RELATIONSHIP.
SOMETIMES IT'S NICE TO LET SOMEONE ELSE TAKE CARE OF THEM FOR A CHANGE.
"DID ANYTHING OUT OF THE ORDINARY HAPPEN AT THE FUNDRAISER?"
"KIND OF. *DOGFACE REILLY* TRIED TO STEAL THE MONEY."
NOBODY MOVE. THIS IS A STICK-UP!

HERE WE GO.
HAPPENS EVERY TIME...
HEY, THAT'S NOT DOGFACE REILLY!

HE'S WEARING A MASK!
I AM TOO DOGFACE REILLY!

"IT WAS THE HEAD OF THE SCHOOL DISTRICT. HE WAS ROBBING HIS OWN CHARITY EVENT TO COVER FOR FUNDS HE'D EMBEZZLED.
"HE WAS SO NERVOUS AND SWEATY, THE MASK SLIPPED OFF HIS HEAD.
"IT WASN'T EVEN A REAL GUN."

"SO THE CAT WAS NOT SEEN IN PUBLIC ANYWHERE THAT NIGHT."
"NOPE."

"THEN WHY WERE YOU IN COSTUME WHEN YOU WERE KILLED?"
"I WAS GOING ON PATROL, JUST LIKE I DO EVERY NIGHT.

"I WAS DROPPED HOME...

"...I WENT UPSTAIRS...

"...AND CHANGED."

"AND THAT'S WHEN IT HAPPENED?"

"THAT'S WHEN IT HAPPENED."
WHO--?

NO ONE.
KLK

BZRRRT

NNNGH!

WH... WHY?
SO MANY QUESTIONS.

THE ANSWERS TO ALL OF THEM SHOULD BE AS OBVIOUS AS A, B...

...C.
"THAT'S THE LAST THING I SAW, HIM TAKING MY MYSTIC RUNE.

"HE TOOK THE SOURCE OF MY SUPER POWERS, AND HE TOOK MY LIFE."

AND THEN APPARENTLY HE TOOK YOUR BODY, BECAUSE IT'S GONE.
PRESUMABLY TO COVER HIS TRACKS.

"NEXT THING I KNOW, I'M IN YOUR APARTMENT, AND I'M A GHOST."
MIRANDA!
AIEEEEEE!
DON'T BE FRIGHTENED. IT'S ME. LINDY.
IT'S YOUR SISTER.
IF THAT'S TRUE, WHY ARE YOU DRESSED LIKE THE CAT AND WHY ARE YOU A GHOST?
BECAUSE I AM THE CAT.
AND BECAUSE I'VE JUST BEEN MURDERED.

THIS IS A LOT TO TAKE IN. W-WHY ARE YOU HERE?
WHY AREN'T YOU HAUNTING THE ZEBRA OR THE ARCHER OR ANY OTHER SUPERHERO?
I DON'T KNOW. THIS IS AS NEW TO ME AS IT IS TO YOU.

MAYBE IT'S BECAUSE WE'RE RELATED BY BLOOD. MAYBE YOU'RE MEANT TO HELP ME SOLVE MY OWN HOMICIDE.

HOW LONG HAVE YOU BEEN THE CAT?
ABOUT SIX YEARS NOW.
A MAN WAS THE CAT BEFORE ME.

"THERE'S AN ANCIENT MAGICAL OBJECT THAT GAVE US OUR FELINE POWERS.
"ALL TWENTY-SIX MEMBERS OF THE ALPHABET GUILD HAS ONE THAT GOES WITH THEIR IDENTITY."

WHEN HE DIED, THE STONE CAME TO ME.
I WAS SUPPOSED TO GIVE IT TO THE NEXT CAT, BUT WHOEVER DID THIS TOOK IT.

MAYBE THAT'S WHY YOU'RE A GHOST. YOU LOST THE RUNE, AND YOU CAN'T SHUFFLE OFF UNTIL YOU FIND A SUCCESSOR.

MAYBE THAT'S *ME!* MAYBE *I'M* GONNA BE THE NEW CAT!

NO, I DON'T THINK SO.
THAT CAN'T BE RIGHT.

WHATEVER REASON THIS PERSON HAD FOR KILLING ME AND TAKING IT...
...THAT'S THE KEY TO SOLVING THIS WHOLE THING.
IT ALL MAKES PERFECT SENSE.

IT'S JUST LIKE YOU SAY, THE STONE HAS TO PASS ON.
I CAN *BE* THE CAT.

NO, YOU CAN'T. THAT'S JUST ASKING FOR TROUBLE.
EXACTLY.
WE WANT TROUBLE.

IMAGINE WHEN THE BAD GUY SEES ME, THINKS IT'S YOU, THINKS YOU'RE ALIVE.
WE WON'T HAVE TO HUNT FOR HIM, HE'LL COME TO US!
"I HAVE YET TO BE PROVEN WRONG."

JUST BECAUSE THEY HAVEN'T COME LOOKING FOR ME *YET* DOESN'T MEAN THEY WON'T.
YOU HAVE MANAGED TO KEEP A FAIRLY LOW PROFILE.
IT'S ONLY A MATTER OF TIME BEFORE SOMEONE I ONCE KNEW CATCHES A GLIMPSE OF YOU.
AND THEN THE HUNTER BECOMES THE HUNTED.
KRASH
WHAT WAS THAT--?
WHOA.
MAYBE I AM SUPER POWERED AFTER ALL.
LIKE I'M PSYCHIC OR HAVE THE POWER OF SUGGESTION.
I *SUMMONED* THE KILLER HERE...

WHO ARE YOU?
WHY ARE YOU DRESSED LIKE THAT?
AND, MOST IMPORTANTLY, WHAT ARE YOU DOING IN MY FRIEND'S APARTMENT?

FRIEND... OR FOE?

CHAPTER 5:
FRIEND OR FOE

GEORGE KAMBADAIS - JAMIE S. RICH

THE DOUBLE LIFE OF MIRANDA TURNER

THE DOUBLE LIFE OF MIRANDA TURNER

Friend or Foe

Written by Jamie S. Rich
Illustrated by George Kambadais
Lettered by Crank!

KONK
OW!

THIS IS LINDY TURNER'S HOUSE.
AND YOU'RE NOT HER.
OBVIOUSLY.

TELL HER WHO YOU ARE!
AND WITH THAT BLACK MASK, I'M GUESSING YOU'RE A BURGLAR.

I'M NOT A BURGLAR...
...I'M THE CAT!

THE CAT WAS MY BEST FRIEND.
YOU'RE NOT *HER* EITHER.

NO! I MEANT TELL HER WHO YOU *REALLY* ARE.
TELL HER YOUR SECRET IDENTITY.

PORTAL IS ONE OF THE FEW PEOPLE WHO KNEW *MINE!*
YOU SHOULDN'T BE HERE, SO PERMIT ME TO ESCORT YOU...
...*OUT* OF THE BUILDING!
HEY! NO FAIR!

YOU TRYING TO KILL ME?
BECAUSE *LINDY* WOULDN'T BE HAPPY WITH YOU...
ZOOP
POP
...IF YOU DID.
YOU KNOW LINDY?
GAH! WHY DO PEOPLE KEEP THROWING ME OUT OF BUILDINGS?

TELL PORTAL YOU'RE MY SISTER!
I TOLD HER ABOUT YOU, SHE JUST DOESN'T KNOW WHAT YOU LOOK LIKE!

I'LL SHOW HER WHAT I LOOK LIKE!
SHOW WHOMMMFFF--

IS THIS ALPHABET GUILD POLICY?
STOP IT, MIRANDA! YOU'RE JUST MAKING IT WORSE!

TOSS PEOPLE AROUND FIRST, ASK QUESTIONS LATER?
GUILD POLICY...

...IS NONE OF YOUR BUSINESS.
OUCH!
POW

DANG!
I THROW A MEAN PUNCH.

YOU'RE IMPERSONATING ONE MISSING PERSON AND BREAKING INTO THE APARTMENT OF ANOTHER.
TELL ME THAT DOESN'T LOOK STRANGE.

NO ONE HAS SEEN THE CAT FOR WEEKS, AND LINDY TURNER FOR ABOUT AS LONG.
THAT HAS NOTHING TO DO WITH ME.

EXCEPT THAT I'M TRYING TO FIND OUT WHAT HAPPENED TO BOTH OF THEM.

IF YOU KNOW SOMETHING...

...YOU SHOULD HAVE INFORMED PROPER AUTHORITIES.
OOF!

THIS ISN'T THE SORT OF THING AMATEURS SHOULD BE POKING THEIR NOSES IN.
THAT'S WHY THERE'S A GUILD.
TO KEEP JUST ANY JANE DOE FROM PUTTING ON A MASK AND CALLING HERSELF A SUPERHERO.
DANG IT, MIRANDA.
WHY WON'T YOU TELL HER THE TRUTH?
BECAUSE I DON'T WANNA.
PORTAL IS THE REAL DEAL.
CRIME-FIGHTING'S THE FAMILY BUSINESS. HER GRANDFATHER WAS IN THE GUILD, TOO.
SO?
WHO ARE YOU TALKING TO?
KABOOM
WHAT THE--?!

YOU DRIVERS REALLY SHOULD KEEP AN EYE OUT FOR LANDMINES.
IT'S LIKE THEY DON'T TRAIN YOU TO DEAL WITH SUPERVILLAINS AT ALL.

EAT LEAD, *CRAB!*
BLAM

HEY, WATCH IT.
NOT EVERYONE HAS A SUPER HARD OUTER SHELL. SOMEONE COULD GET HURT.
KAZING

LIKE YOU, FOR INSTANCE.
I SUGGEST YOU BOYS REGROUP.
TOSS!
WHOMP
GET YOURSELVES TOGETHER...
IT'LL BE ALL RIGHT.
HEH-HEH-HEH.
NOT SO FAST, CRAB.
POW
TIME FOR YOU TO GET SCUTTLED.
WHAM

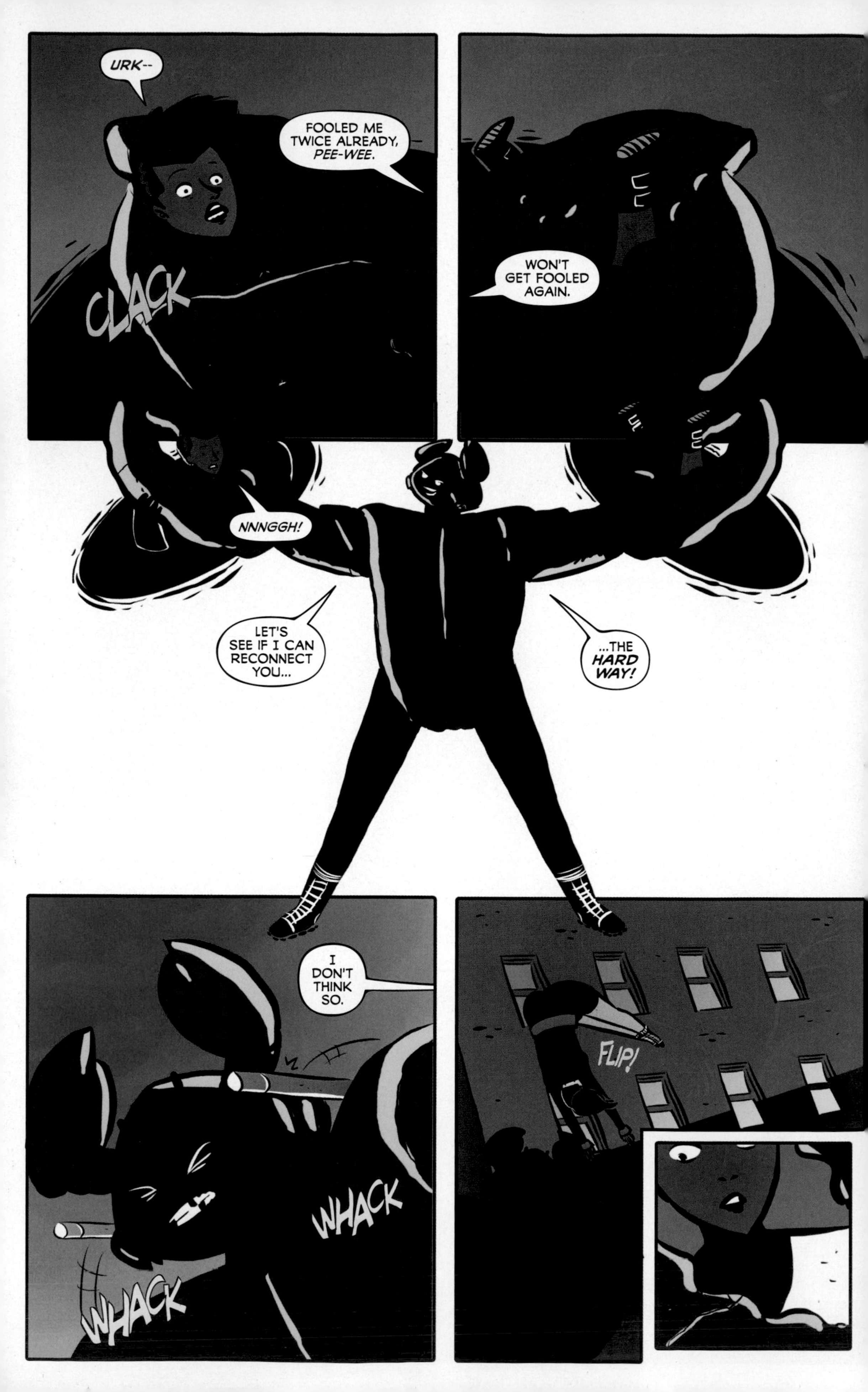
URK--
FOOLED ME TWICE ALREADY, *PEE-WEE*.
CLACK
WON'T GET FOOLED AGAIN.
NNNGGH!
LET'S SEE IF I CAN RECONNECT YOU...
...THE *HARD WAY!*
I DON'T THINK SO.
WHACK
WHACK
FLIP!

NICE WORK.
NOT NICE ENOUGH.
WHO THE--?!
I'M STILL NOT SURE HOW WE'RE GOING TO TAKE THIS BRUTE DOWN.
LOOK!
CRAB BROKE A STEAM PIPE WHEN HE SET OFF THE EXPLOSION TO STOP THE ARMORED CAR.
GRARRRRRRR!
GOOD THINKING, SIS!
GONNA HAVE TO TIME THIS JUST RIGHT...
I'LL POP YOUR HEAD CLEAN--

--OWWWWFFFFFFF!
WHO'S UP FOR A SEAFOOD BOIL?
HA!
FWOOSH

Not long after...
I HAVE TO ADMIT, THAT WAS FAST THINKING.
KIND OF FUNNY, TOO, GIVEN ALL THE HOLES YOU OPENED, THAT HE FELL INTO MINE.

GO AHEAD AND TAKE ALL THE CREDIT.
NEXT THING, YOU'LL BE TELLING HER YOU POURED THE CONCRETE, TOO.
GEEZ, YOU'RE A NAG!

ME?
I WAS COMPLIMENTING YOU!

SORRY. I DON'T MEAN YOU.
THIS IS AWKWARD.
LISTEN, I HAVE SOMETHING I NEED TO TELL YOU.

GUILTY CONSCIENCE, EH?
FINALLY READY TO CONFESS?
IN A MANNER OF SPEAKING.
ABOUT THE CAT AND LINDY TURNER...

...WE BOTH KNOW THAT THEY'RE BOTH MISSING BECAUSE THEY'RE THE SAME PERSON.
SHHHH! NOT SO LOUD!
I'M NOT SAYING YOU'RE RIGHT, BUT HOW DO YOU KNOW THIS?

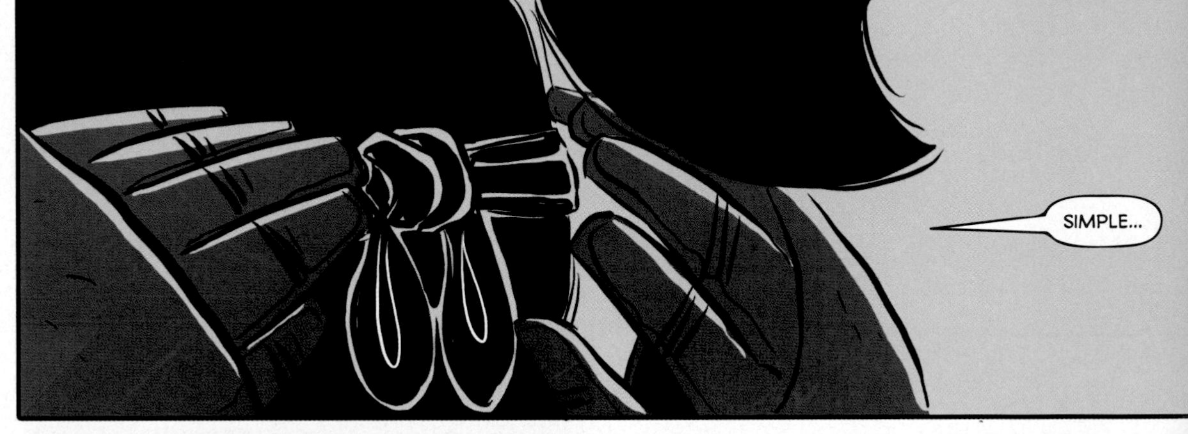
SIMPLE...

I'M MIRANDA TURNER.
I'M LINDY'S SISTER.

FOR GOODNESS SAKE!
WHY DIDN'T YOU SAY SO?
THAT'S WHAT LINDY KEEPS ASKING ME.

LINDY?! YOU'VE TALKED TO HER?
YOU KNOW WHERE SHE IS?!

AS A MATTER OF FACT...
SHE'S BEEN HERE THE WHOLE TIME.

CHAPTER 6:
PAST MASTERS

GEORGE KAMBADAIS - JAMIE S. RICH

THE DOUBLE LIFE OF MIRANDA TURNER #6

YOU SHOULD HAVE SPOKEN UP EARLIER, *MIRANDA*.
LINDY MENTIONED YOU TO ME.
THAT'S WHAT I SAID!
GAWD, I'M IN FOR A NEVER-ENDING "I TOLD YOU SO."
THE DOUBLE LIFE OF MIRANDA TURNER
"PAST MASTERS"
WRITTEN BY JAMIE S. RICH
ILLUSTRATED BY GEORGE KAMBADAIS
LETTERED BY CRANK!

WELL, FOR WHAT IT'S WORTH, YOU HANDLED YOURSELF WELL WITH *CRAB*.
YOUR SISTER SHOULD BE PROUD THAT YOU TOOK OVER BEING *THE CAT*.

YEAH, SHE'S NOT TOO HAPPY ABOUT THAT EITHER.
THE SUPERHERO IDENTITY NOT BEING *OFFICIAL* AND ALL.

OH, TRUST ME, I KNOW WHAT IT'S LIKE HAVING LINDY ON YOUR BACK.
HEY!
WHAT'S THAT SUPPOSED TO MEAN?
DON'T FRET. JUST BECAUSE THE ALPHABET GUILD HASN'T RECRUITED YOU YET, DOESN'T MEAN THEY WON'T.
YOU COULD BE A LEGACY HERO, JUST LIKE ME.
A LEGACY HERO?
EGADS, DON'T ENCOURAGE HER.

YEAH, YOU KNOW. PART OF A LINEAGE OF HEROES.
KEEPIN' IT IN THE FAMILY.
FUNNILY ENOUGH, MY GRANDFATHER USED TO BE THE CAT.
NO WAY!
ABSOLUTELY. ONE BEFORE THE GUY WHO WAS BEFORE LINDY...

"...BACK IN THE 1960s.
"HE WAS SPECIALLY CONSCRIPTED INTO THE ARMY TO SERVE IN THE VIETNAM WAR.

"FROM THE LETTERS HE SENT, THE COMBAT SOUNDED AS HAIRY AS THEY MAKE IT LOOK IN THE MOVIES."
SWEET UNCLE SAM!
IT'S AN AMBUSH!

"HE FOUGHT SIDE-BY-SIDE WITH THE REGULAR JOES, PUTTING HIS LIFE IN DANGER JUST LIKE ANY OL' GRUNT."
SHP
WHACK
POW

"THOUGH, HE HAD ONE ADDED DANGER."

STMP KRSH

"ONE HE WAS PERHAPS SPECIALLY EQUIPPED FOR."

UH-OH.

"THE NORTH VIETNAMESE HAD THEIR OWN SUPERPOWERED WEAPON.

"MY GRANDFATHER'S NEMESIS.

"*THE STONE MAN OF ANGKOR WAT*.

"HE AND MY GRANDFATHER TUSSLED AGAIN AND AGAIN..."
POW

POW
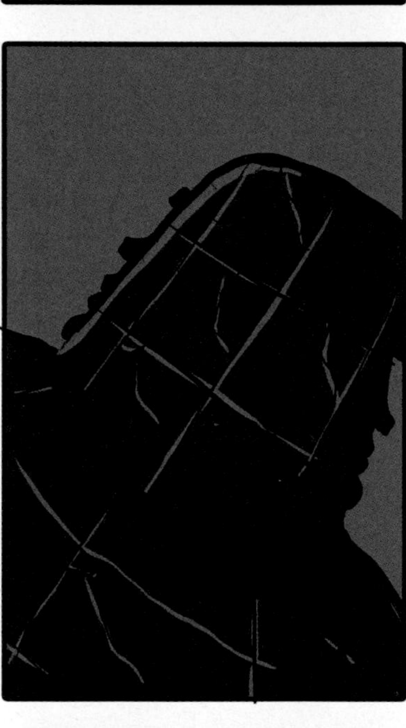

KRAK

URK!
"WE DON'T KNOW IF THE STONE MAN WAS RESPONSIBLE FOR HIS DEATH..."

...OR IF HE EVEN DIED AT ALL.
ALL WE KNOW IS THAT GRANDPA NEVER CAME BACK.

HE MUST'VE DIED. THAT'S WHEN MY PREDECESSOR TOOK OVER THE ROLE OF CAT.
WAS YOUR FATHER AN ALPHABET, TOO?

NO, IT SKIPPED A GENERA--

--TION.
OH, MY.

PORTAL?
YOU OKAY?

SOMETHING'S HAPPENING.
SOMEONE'S *HERE!*

HOLY CALAMITY!

SOMETHING TELLS ME THAT'S THE RIGHT NOUN, BUT THE WRONG ADJECTIVE.
HEY, PORTAL, CAN YOU...

...GET US OVER THERE?
SHE'S GONE.

SHE MUST ALREADY BE ON HER WAY.
WE BETTER GET MOVING SO WE DON'T KEEP HER WAITING.

WHAT IS IT?
WERE PEOPLE STILL INSIDE?
THE MAYOR JUST GOT HERE.

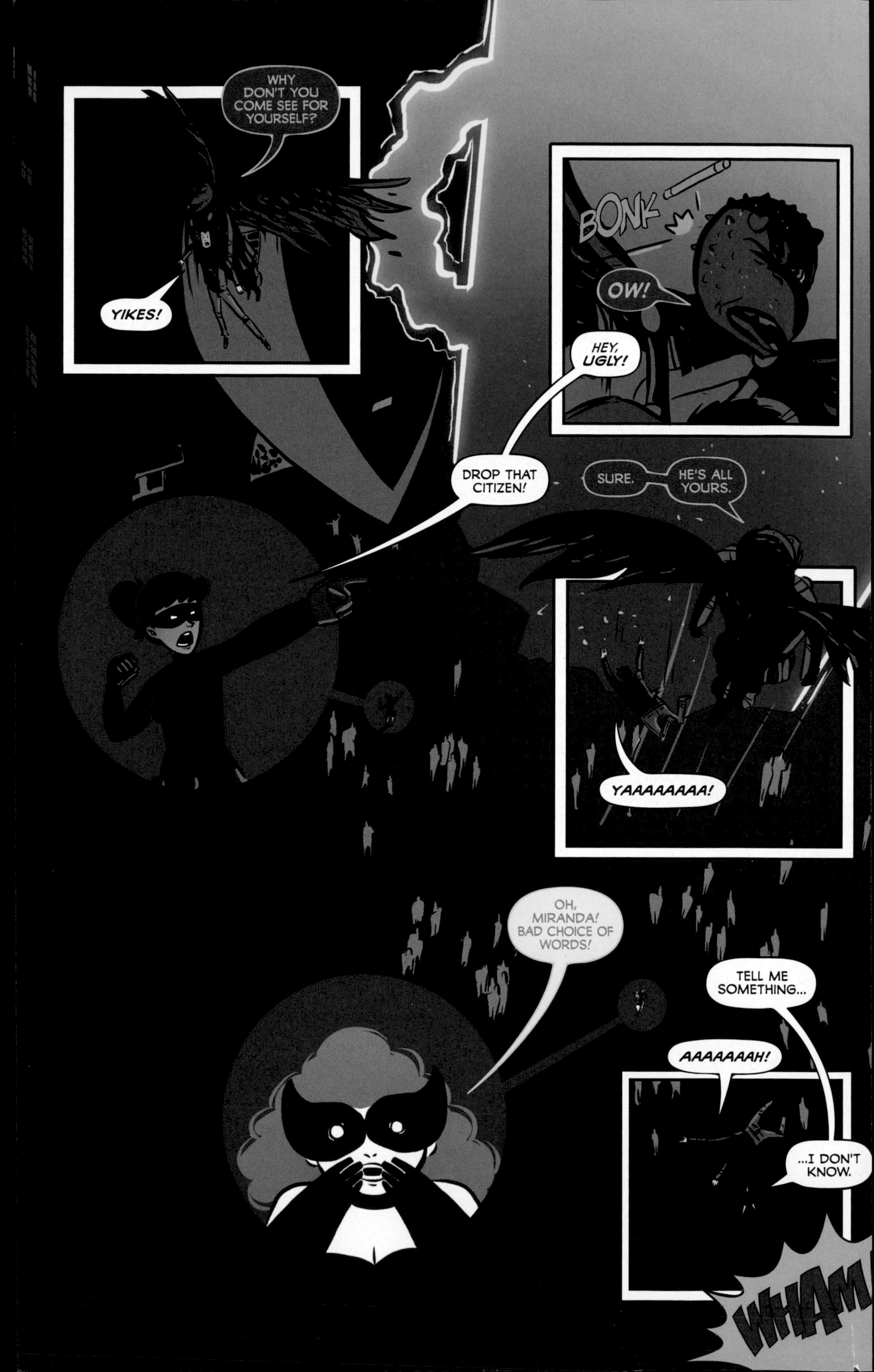
WHY DON'T YOU COME SEE FOR YOURSELF?
YIKES!
BONK
OW!
HEY, UGLY!
DROP THAT CITIZEN!
SURE.
HE'S ALL YOURS.
YAAAAAAAA!
OH, MIRANDA! BAD CHOICE OF WORDS!
TELL ME SOMETHING...
AAAAAAAH!
...I DON'T KNOW.
WHAM

YOU ALL RIGHT, SIR?
I THINK SO...
CLAP
CLAP
CLAP
CLAP
CLAP

CLAP
CLAP
BRAVO!
A TREMENDOUS PERFORMANCE.

I HOPE SOMEONE FILMED THAT, IT'LL MAKE A HILARIOUS ANIMATED .GIF.
TENGU!

IS IT PRONOUNCED "GIFF" OR "JIFF," I'VE NEVER BEEN SURE?
ANYONE?

FWISH
NEVER MIND.
I WASN'T REALLY ASKING YOU ANYWAY.

YAHHH!
WHAT DID YOU DO TO THEM?

NOTHING MUCH.
FOO
--!
I MERELY FROZE THEM OUT OF THE EQUATION.

NOW, YOU, YOU'RE NOT THE CAT, ARE YOU, CHILD?
UH... OF COURSE I AM.

NO, YOU'RE NOT.
I CAN SAY SO DEFINITIVELY, BECAUSE...

...SHE IS!
GASP!
NOW I KNOW YOU'RE JUST CRAZY.
ANYONE WITH TWO EYES CAN SEE THERE'S NOTHING THERE.
IT'S NO USE. IT'S THAT MASK OF HIS.
HE'S GOT POWERS.
SHE SPEAKS THE TRUTH, YOUNG LADY.
YOU SHOULD LISTEN TO HER.
AND THEN YOU SHOULD LISTEN TO ME.
YOU WANT NO PART OF THIS, YOU BIG FAKER.
TO MAKE A TURN ON AN OLD PHRASE...
...YOU'RE NOT BIG ENOUGH FOR THIS TOWN.
NOT UNDER ITS NEW MANAGEMENT.

DEAD CAT.
COPYCAT.
ALLOW ME TO INTRODUCE MY ASSOCIATES...

...THE DAEMON GENTRY!

BRETHREN, THE CITY--
--AND ITS PEOPLE--
--ARE *YOURS*.

Chapter 7:
Daemon Days

GEORGE KAMBADAIS - JAMIE S. RICH

THE DOUBLE LIFE OF MIRANDA TURNER

#7

KAMBADAIS 2015

THAT'S QUITE AN INTERESTING STATE YOU'VE GOTTEN YOURSELF INTO.
DID YOU FAIL TO COMPLETELY USE UP YOUR NINE LIVES?
IS *THIS* THE RESIDUE?

A few minutes from now...
IF I COULD *TOUCH* YOU, CAT--
--AND NOT JUST *CONTAIN* YOU--
--I'D FINISH THE JOB.

I'D LIKE TO SEE YOU TRY, TENGU!
WHMP

WHY? SO YOU CAN SEE ME FAIL?
I RESPECT MY LIMITATIONS, CAT, ALWAYS HAVE.

YOU KNOW THAT. IF I CAN'T WIN ONE WAY...
...I WIN ANOTHER.
IF I CAN'T KILL YOU...
NO!
...I'LL KILL YOUR IMPOSTER.

THE DOUBLE LIFE OF MIRANDA TURNER

"DAEMON DAYS"

WRITTEN BY JAMIE S. RICH
ILLUSTRATED BY GEORGE KAMBADAIS
LETTERED BY CRANK!

Back at the start...

...BECAUSE WE MAY BE IN OVER OUR HEADS HERE.

LADIES, THERE IS NO SENSE IN DAWDLING.

WHETHER OR NOT YOU ENTER OF YOUR OWN VOLITION...
WHAT THE--?

POP
...YOU *WILL* COME INSIDE.

WHY MAKE US WAIT?

NOW, LET ME INTRODUCE YOU TO THE NEW RULING CLASS.
ADROGANS, THE CONCEITED.
AUGUSTUS, THE PETTY.
AND IN THE MIDDLE...
...DOMINARI, THE TERRIBLE.
COLLECTIVELY, THE DAEMON GENTRY.
THEM BOYS BE UGLY.
YOU SAY THAT NOW, BUT JUST WAIT.
PRETTY SOON, EVERYONE WILL WANT TO LOOK LIKE THEM.
I MEAN, TAKE A GANDER, COPYCAT.
THERE'S A LINE OUTSIDE...

...JUST DYING TO BE PART OF THE IN-CROWD.
POP
YOU'RE INSANE, TENGU.
YOU'LL NEVER GET AWAY WITH THIS.
WHO HERE'S GOING TO STOP ME?
YOUR COSTUMED FRIENDS HAVEN'T COME TO YOUR RESCUE.
"OUR PERIMETER IS GROWING BY THE MINUTE, AND YET, THE WORLD AT LARGE IS OBLIVIOUS TO ITS CREEPING DOOM.
"WE HAVE CLOSED THEIR EYES TO THE TRUTH.
"LIKE A VIDEO CAMERA LOOPED TO SHOW THE SAME PICTURE, WE PROJECT AN OUTWARD VISION OF PEACE AND QUIET.
"PEOPLE CAN ONLY SEE IT COMING WHEN IT'S ALREADY TOO LATE."

SO, YOU SEE, ALL THERE IS BETWEEN US AND WORLD DOMINATION...
...IS A DEAD GIRL AND A PRETENDER TO THE MASK.
THEN I GUESS YOU'RE *SCREWED,* AIN'TCHA?
GACK!
TAKE A KNEE, PAL.
OOF!
MAN, I THOUGHT HE'D *NEVER* SHUT UP.
WAIT!
YOU CAN'T RUSH INTO THIS.
THERE'S TOO MANY OF THEM.
KRAK
POW
IT'S ALL TOO MUCH.
IF NOT ME, THEN WHO?

YOU HEARD HIM. NO ONE ELSE IS COMING.

YOU HAVE TO TAKE THIS SERIOUSLY.
I KNOW IT SEEMS FUN TO PUT ON THE MASK--

I'VE TAKEN THIS SERIOUSLY FROM DAY ONE.
DON'T CONFUSE *YOUR* NOT GIVING ME ANY CREDIT WITH ME GOOFING AROUND.

I GIVE YOU CREDIT!
I SHOULD HOPE SO.
YOU'RE THE ONE WHO ASKED ME TO HELP YOU SOLVE YOUR MURDER.

AND I APPRECIATE IT, BUT I'VE PUSHED YOU IN OVER YOUR HEAD.
I'VE LET YOU PLAY AROUND--
I'M *NOT* PLAYING!
WHACK

YES, YOU *ARE*.
YOU THINK THIS IS ANOTHER ACTING ROLE.
SMACK

THAT ALL IT TAKES IS A COSTUME AND MAKEUP AND A FEW WITTY LINES, AND YOU'RE A SUPERHERO.

EXCEPT YOU'RE *NOT*.
BOOF

DURSH
YOU'RE JUST AN ACTRESS.

YEAH?
AND YOU WERE "JUST" A MODEL.
THAT'S NOT FAIR, I HAD--
HAD WHAT? A PRETTY FACE?
THE CLOTHES THEY GAVE YOU?
LOOK HOW PLAYING DRESS-UP WORKED OUT FOR YOU-- URRKK!

YOU TWO TALK TOO MUCH.
IT'S A RIDICULOUSLY *HUMAN* TRAIT.

I THOUGHT WAS GOING TO LIKE THIS GIRL WHEN SHE GOT TENGU TO PIPE DOWN.
BUT THEN SHE JUST FILLED THE VOID WITH HER OWN PRATTLE.

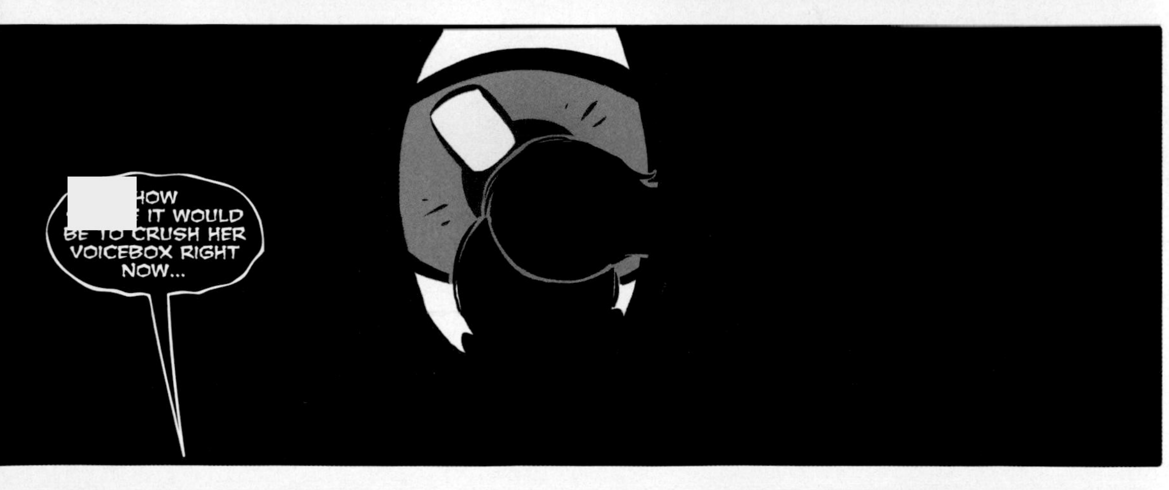
HOW IT WOULD BE TO CRUSH HER VOICEBOX RIGHT NOW...

...BUT EVEN THAT WOULD BE MORE EFFORT THAN SHE'S WORTH.
FLICK

NO!

I'M BORED WITH THIS.

HANG ON, BABY SISTER.
I'M GOING TO TAKE OVER YOUR BODY AND GET YOU OUT OF HERE.

NOT SO FAST!
ZPOP

LET ME GO!
IF I CAN'T WIN ONE WAY...
...I'LL WIN ANOTHER.

IF I CAN'T KILL *YOU*...

...THEN I'LL KILL YOUR COPYCAT!

Chapter 8:
Take Me to the Other Side

GEORGE KAMBADAIS - JAMIE S. RICH

THE DOUBLE LIFE OF MIRANDA TURNER #8

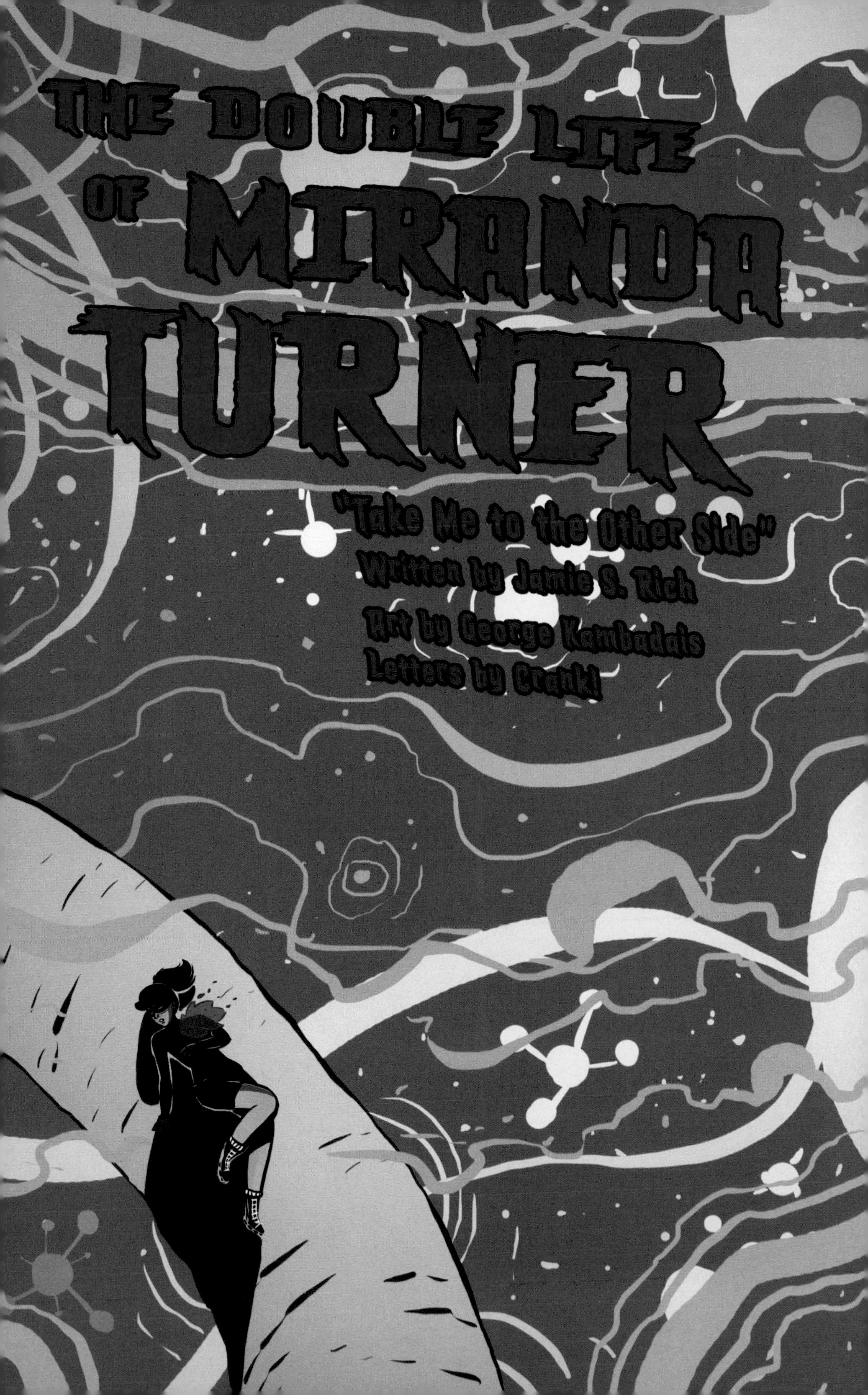
THE DOUBLE LIFE OF MIRANDA TURNER
"Take Me to the Other Side"
Written by Jamie S. Rich
Art by George Kambadais
Letters by Crank!

HELLO...?
DID TENGU KILL ME?
AM I DEAD NOW, TOO?
NO.
NOT YET AT LEAST.
BUT YOU ARE NOW SEPARATE.
SEPARATE FROM YOUR WORLD, SEPARATE FROM YOUR SISTER.
SEPARATE FROM YOURSELF.
ARE YOU THE ONE...

...WHO KILLED LINDY?
ME?
NO...

I WAS DEAD MYSELF LONG BEFORE THAT.

IF I HADN'T BEEN...WELL, THINGS WOULD HAVE BEEN VERY DIFFERENT FOR YOUR SISTER.
YOU'RE THE CAT!

ONE OF THEM, YES.
FOR OVER THREE DECADES. LONGER THAN ANY OTHER.

HOW DID YOU DIE?
WAS IT YOUR ARCH-NEMESIS? SPACE ALIENS?
PLANE CRASH, IRONICALLY ENOUGH.

"AFTER ALL THE IMPOSSIBLE AND DANGEROUS THINGS I DID IN LIFE, MY DEATH WAS JUST A STROKE OF BAD LUCK."
LADIES AND GENTLEMAN, PLEASE ADOPT A CRASH POSITION...

"BUT THEN, WE CATS ARE ONLY STRONG, NOT INVINCIBLE."

YEAH, I HEARD HOW PORTAL'S GRANDFATHER DIED.
DID YOU MEET HIM?
NOT PERSONALLY, NO.

NOT EVEN HERE... ON THE OTHER SIDE?
IT'S A BIG PLACE.
AND YOU'RE THE ONE WITH THE TALENT FOR SEEING GHOSTS.

ANYWAY, YOU'RE PART OF A HEROIC TRADITION NOW.

I'M NOT A ***CAT***. I JUST DRESS LIKE ONE.
PERHAPS.
THE RUNE GIVES US POWER, BUT THE IDENTITY... ***THAT'S*** UP TO YOU.

FUNNY THING...
NOW THAT I'M HERE, IT GIVES ME CAUSE TO WONDER JUST ***WHO*** I AM.

"WHEN WE WERE BATTLING *TENGU*, LINDY ACCUSED ME OF TREATING CRIMEFIGHTING AS JUST ANOTHER ACTING ROLE.
"EVEN WHEN I THINK BACK TO WHEN WE WERE KIDS, IT WAS THE SAME.
"LINDY WAS ALWAYS WHO SHE WAS...
"...I ALWAYS ADAPTED AND BECAME OTHER PEOPLE."
I KNOW SO WELL WHAT BECOMES OF UNMARRIED WOMEN WHO AREN'T PREPARED TO OCCUPY A POSITION.
YOU SAY THAT LIKE IT'S A BAD THING.
ISN'T IT?
MAYBE THERE'S A REASON THE RUNE DIDN'T CHOOSE YOU. YOU EVER CONSIDER THAT?
IT WAS LOST. *STOLEN*.
SO TO SPEAK.

OR MAYBE YOU DON'T ***NEED*** WHAT IT HAS TO OFFER.
LINDY WAS CHOSEN FOR HER CONFIDENCE AND BRAVERY.
DON'T YOU WORRY, LITTLE LADY.
AH'M HEAH TO SAVE YOU.
GOT TO GET TO HIGHER GROUND!
YOU WANT ME TO GET YOUR HORSE IN POSITION?
RRAR?

WHEN COWBOYS JUMP OUT OF SALOON WINDOWS...
...IT DOESN'T LOOK *THIS* HIGH.
SIGH
TUNK!

I GUESS THIS TIME THE PRINCESS HAS TO SAVE THE COWBOY, *EH?*
YOU SEE? SHE HAD YOUR BEST INTERESTS IN MIND.
YOUR POWER LIES IN YOUR EMPATHY.
YOU CAN SEE YOURSELF IN OTHER PEOPLE, AND THAT OPENS YOU TO INSIGHTS OTHERS DON'T HAVE.
CLAP CLAP CLAP CLAP
CLAP CLAP CLAP CLAP

FORGET HIM, LINDY.
HE'S A JERK.
YEAH...
OH, MIRANDA.
I'M SO SORRY. THIS WAS SUPPOSED TO BE *YOUR* NIGHT.

PSHAW. DON'T GIVE IT ANOTHER THOUGHT.
I ALREADY GOT MY APPLAUSE.
I COULD NEVER DO WHAT YOU DO, MIRANDA, STAND UP IN FRONT OF ALL THOSE PEOPLE.
YOU'D BE SURPRISED WHAT A DIFFERENCE A COSTUME MAKES.
IT'S LIKE NO ONE KNOWS ME.
LINDY, YOU CAN HIDE IN PLAIN SIGHT.
HEY, YOU GUYS!
TURN ON THE TELEVISION. YOU HAVE TO SEE THIS!

IT HAPPENED JUST AROUND THE CORNER.
THE CAT SAVED THE DAY!
SUPERHERO FOILS ROBBERY! AND WE HAVE THE FOOTAGE...
HOW COOL WOULD IT BE TO BUMP INTO HER? SHE'S THE BEST!
YOU SEE WHAT I MEAN?
I THINK SO.
I'M A PART OF THIS REGARDLESS OF MY OFFICIAL ROLE.
THE CAT RUNE'S POWERS ARE MANY.
MAYBE IT CHOSE YOU TO HELP YOUR SISTER, OR MAYBE IT KNEW YOU ALREADY HAD IT WITHIN YOU TO DO SO.

WHAT DO YOU MEAN?
DON'T YOU FIND IT ODD THAT THE ONLY PEOPLE WHO COULD SEE HER BESIDES YOU HAD SOME KIND OF MYSTICAL POWER?
I HAVEN'T HAD TIME TO THINK ABOUT IT...
OR THAT TENGU'S RITUAL SACRIFICE CAUSED YOU TO END UP HERE RATHER THAN DYING?
OMINOUS OMENS, STRANGE TURNS OF EVENT...
SOMETHING IS HAPPENING, AND IT MUST BE STOPPED.
POP
NOT BY *YOU*, DEAD MAN!

THIS ONE IS *MINE*.
AND NO ONE WILL SHUFFLE HER OFF THIS MORTAL COIL BUT *ME*.

LET'S SEE JUST HOW MANY TIMES...

...A CAT CAN DIE!

Chapter 9:
Spitting Out the Demons

GEORGE KAMBADAIS - JAMIE S. RICH

THE DOUBLE LIFE OF MIRANDA TURNER

#9

KAMBADAIS 2015

PITY THIS *CAT* WILL NEVER BE MORE THAN A KITTEN.
HER YOUNG LIFE CUT SHORT.
HAD YOU KNOWN HER LONG?
YOU'RE A MONSTER, *TENGU*.
IN FACT, THAT MASK OF YOURS IS A LIE.
IT MAKES YOU LOOK *LESS* HIDEOUS THAN YOU REALLY ARE.
SNORT

BE THAT AS IT MAY, THE MORAL COMPASS OF THIS TOWN IS TURNING *MY* WAY.

SOMEONE *GOOD* HAD TO BE SACRIFICED...

...TO MAKE WAY FOR A WHOLE LOT OF *BAD*.

THE DOUBLE LIFE OF MIRANDA TURNER
"SPITTING OUT THE DEMONS"
WRITTEN BY JAMIE S. RICH
ILLUSTRATED BY GEORGE KAMBADAIS
LETTERED BY CRANK!
AH!
I WOULDN'T START DOING A VICTORY LAP JUST YET, TENGU.

WHOMP
FRANKLY, I DON'T KNOW HOW MY SISTER PUT UP WITH YOU AS HER ARCH-NEMESIS FOR SO LONG.

THIS IS MY FIRST TIME MEETING YOU, AND I'M ALREADY SICK OF YOU.
POP!
KIDDO! YOU'RE OKAY!

OF COURSE!
I WAS SO WORRIED ABOUT YOU.

HOW MANY NINE LIVES JOKES DOES EACH CAT GET?
I THINK THIS IS MY FIRST LEGITIMATE NARROW ESCAPE.

IMPOSSIBLE.
I BANISHED YOUR SOUL TO LIMBO.

I GUESS YOU COULD SAY I WAS ABLE TO WIGGLE BACK IN UNDER THE STICK.
GET IT? "LIMBO."
DID I COME OUT OF *THAT?*
THAT'S SO WEIRD. IT'S LIKE I CLIMBED OUT OF MY OWN SKIN.
YOUR FAILURE HAS LEFT A RIFT BETWEEN DIMENSIONS, TENGU.
YOU WOULD HAVE US PRETEND YOU ARE DAEMON GENTRY...
...BUT THEN YOU SUBJECT US TO *HUMAN* ERROR.
NO...
NO.

I CAN FIX THIS.
OUR EXISTENCE ON THIS PLANE HAS BEEN COMPROMISED.

THIS CITY HAS BEEN PROMISED TO YOU.
THIS *EARTH*.

PROMISED BY *ME*. SO YOU COULD TRANSFORM THIS MORTAL SHELL INTO ONE OF YOUR OWN...
...JUST AS YOU WOULD TRANSFORM THIS LAND AND ITS PEOPLE.

YOU SEEK POWER THAT YOU ARE ILL EQUIPPED TO HANDLE.
AND HERE *I* AM MEANT TO BE THE ARROGANT ONE.

I CAN HANDLE POWER JUST FINE.
I MERELY NEED TO RECLAIM IT.

I WANT YOU TO PONDER THE IRONY, TENGU, OF A WOULD-BE DEMON...

...BEING *POSSESSED* BY A GHOST.
URK!

IS THIS WHAT YOU WERE AFTER?
HE CAN'T DO ANYTHING. NOW HE TRULY *IS* POWERLESS.
LITTLE GIRL, YOU DON'T REALIZE WHAT YOU'RE PLAYING WITH.
REALLY? IS THIS THING DANGEROUS?

MAYBE I SHOULD SEND IT BACK TO NEVER-NEVER LAND?

NO, *WAIT!*
YOU'LL ONLY DOOM YOURSELF!

JUDGING BY WHAT TENGU IS THINKING, THE FAT ONE IS LYING.
THEY *REALLY* DON'T WANT YOU TO DO THAT.

OOPSIE.

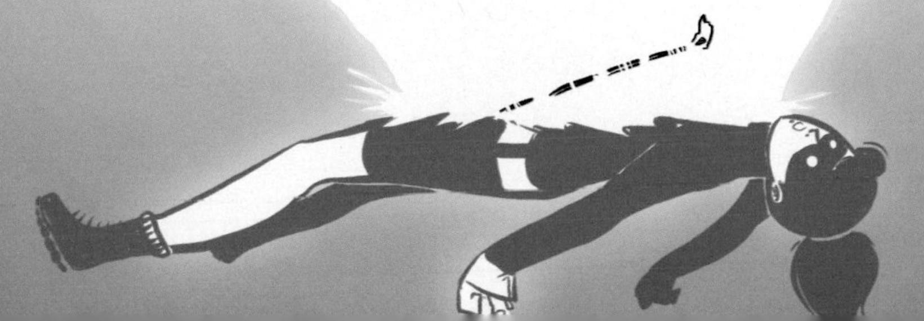

SKKKKKKKK
KKKKKKKKSSS
RIGHT. WE'RE UNDONE.
NOT JUST US...

I'LL ENJOY SPENDING ETERNITY TORTURING THIS ONE.
JUMP BACK!
I DON'T THINK SO.
TENGU IS A HUMAN. HE'S OURS TO PUNISH, NOT YOURS.
NOT TO MENTION HE'S STILL POSSESSED BY MY SISTER, AND I CAN'T RISK YOU TAKING HER TO HELL WITH YOU.
FINE. THREE FOR THE PRICE OF ONE.
ERRR, BOSS...
UH-OH.

SKKKKKK
NOOOOOOO
SHWP
KRK

WHAT HAPPENED?
I DON'T KNOW, BUT YOU LOOKED PRETTY FREAKY.
SPEAK FOR YOURSELF...

READY?
ON THE COUNT OF THREE.
ONE... TWO--

THREE!
POW

LOOKS LIKE EVERYONE'S ALL RIGHT, EVEN IF A TAD WORSE FOR WEAR.
YOU DID A GOOD THING TODAY, MIRANDA.
YOU WERE A REAL HERO.
NOT ONLY DID YOU SAVE ALL THESE PEOPLE FROM BECOMING SLAVES TO DEMONS...
...BUT YOU PUT YOURSELF IN HARM'S WAY TO PROTECT THE BAD GUY.
IT JUST SEEMED LIKE THE RIGHT THING TO DO.
IT *WAS*. AND YOU SAVED ME AT THE SAME TIME.
MAYBE YOU HAVE WHAT IT TAKES TO BE A CRIMEFIGHTER AFTER ALL...
...*CAT*.

I DON'T KNOW, SIS.
I'VE BARELY HAD TIME TO BREATHE IN THE LAST SEVERAL DAYS.
IS THE HERO BIZ ALWAYS THIS FAST-PACED?
I'M AFRAID SO.
NO REST FOR THE WICKED MEANS THE GOOD GUYS DON'T GET TO TAKE ANY BREAKS, EITHER.
YOU KNOW THERE'S STILL TIME TO BACK OUT RIGHT?
I WON'T HOLD IT AGAINST YOU.
NO WAY!
NOT AFTER ALL THE EFFORT IT TOOK JUST TO GET YOU TO ACCEPT ME WEARING THE MASK.
BESIDES, WE STILL HAVE A KILLER TO CATCH...

"I SAW SOME THINGS IN LIMBO.
I SAW THE MAN WE'RE AFTER.
"HE'S STILL OUT THERE.
AND HE'S WATCHING US."

END VOLUME 1

MERRY CHRISTMAS

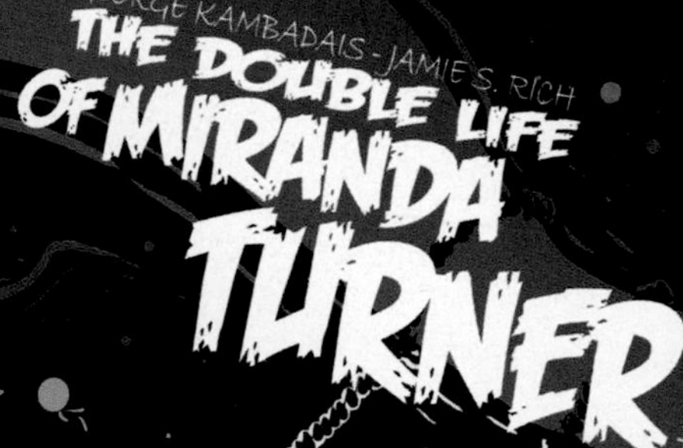

THE DOUBLE LIFE OF MIRANDA TURNER!

By George Kambadais

Above: Various drawings and part of the original *Miranda Turner* webcomic by George Kambadais.

Next Page: The afterword from *The Double Life of Miranda Turner* #1.

HELLO, KITTIES.

Welcome to *The Double Life of Miranda Turner.*

When I got an e-mail from George Kambadais just a few short months ago, I had no idea what was in store. He had been sent my way by David Lafuente, a pretty great artist in his own right whose work on *Patsy Walker: Hellcat* and *Ultimate Spider-Man*, for my money, is some of the best cape-and-cowl artwork to have hit the stands in recent memory.

I was already a fan of George's and had been following him on Tumblr. Naturally, I jumped at the chance to collaborate with him.

The Double Life of Miranda Turner was a concept he had toyed with on his own that he was looking to flesh out. The core idea of two sisters, one of whom had been a superhero, died, and came back as a ghost to enlist the other in finding her killer, proved irresistible, and I immediately sent George some ideas for places the story could go, including possible outcomes of the murder mystery and what will become of Miranda after she's figured it all out.

Once I had the thumbs up from George, it was full steam ahead.

And from the get-go, we hoped we could publish it through Monkeybrain. Chris and Allison have made quite a splash with their operation, and their roster of titles would mean Miranda would be in esteemed company. I love the immediacy of the straight-to-digital model. I've never had a comic come together with such ease.

We all hope you stick around to see where Miranda and Lindy are heading. This first issue was designed to be a fun introduction to the girls and the world they live in, but rest assured, we have a plan here. Our two Cats have a lot more adventures in store.

- Jamie S. Rich
Portland, OR
September 29, 2013

GEORGE KAMBADAIS is a freelance comic artist whose previous work includes *The Vampire Diaries* #4, published by DC Comics; *A Place in the Heart*, published digitally by Stela; and *Rudolph the Red-Nosed Reindeer: The Island of Misfit Toys*, published by Square Fish. He lives in Greece and regularly updates his art blog with new drawings at **gkambadais.com**. Follow him on Twitter **@GeorgeKambadais**.

JAMIE S. RICH is an author whose venues include Oni Press, Image Comics, and Dark Horse. He is best known for his collaborations with artist Joëlle Jones on the graphic novels *12 Reasons Why I Love Her* and *You Have Killed Me*. He published his first prose novel, *Cut My Hair*, in 2000, and his first superhero comic book, *It Girl and the Atomics*, in 2012. Most recently, he worked with Joëlle Jones again on the Eisner-nominated *Lady Killer* series.
www.confessions123.com @jamieESrich

PAULINA GANUCHEAU is a comic artist and illustrator located in Maryland. She is the co-creator of *Zodiac Starforce*.
Her hobbies include watching pro wrestling, cloud photography, and following cats on Instagram.
paulinaganucheau.tumblr.com @PlinaGanucheau

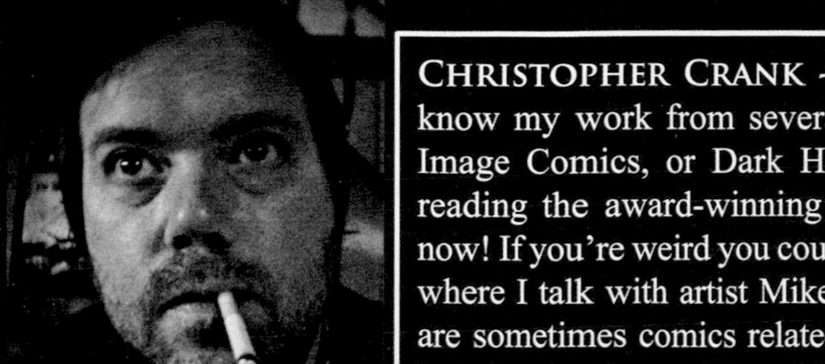

CHRISTOPHER CRANK - Hi! I go by Crank! You might know my work from several recent books from Oni Press, Image Comics, or Dark Horse. Heck, you might even be reading the award-winning *Battlepug* (battlepug.com) right now! If you're weird you could have heard me at **crankcast.net** where I talk with artist Mike Norton weekly about things that are sometimes comics related. If you're super obscure you've heard me play music with the Vladimirs or Sono Morti (**sonomorti.bandcamp.com**). Catch me on Twitter: **@ccrank**.

MORE BOOKS FROM JAMIE S. RICH AND IMAGE COMICS

IT GIRL & THE ATOMICS, VOL. 1
Jamie S. Rich, Mike Norton, & Chynna Clugston Flores
168 Pages * Softcover
Full Color Interiors
ISBN 978-1-607067-25-2

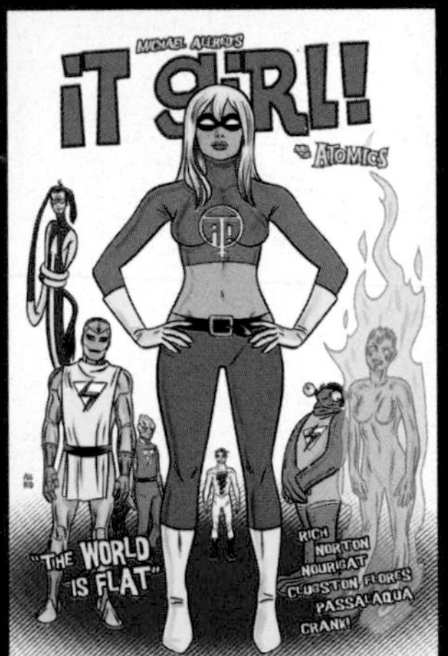

IT GIRL & THE ATOMICS, VOL. 2
Jamie S. Rich, Mike Norton, Natalie Nourigat, & Chynna Clugston Flores
168 Pages * Softcover
Full Color Interiors
ISBN 978-1-607067-91-7

MADAME FRANKENSTEIN
Jamie S. Rich, Megan Levens
192 pages * Softcover
Black-and-white interiors
ISBN: 978-1-632151-97-1